I tore the whiskey bottle from Dad's hand and ran into the kitchen. Then I started dumping the booze down the sink.

Dad yanked me around and pulled the bottle away from me. "What are you doing, Darcy?" he shouted. "Give me that bottle!"

"You're nothing but a drunk!" I cried. "I hate you. I'll hate you forever!"

There's No Cure

There's No Cure

Shannon Kennedy

cover photo by John Strange

Published by Willowisp Press, Inc.
401 E. Wilson Bridge Road, Worthington, Ohio 43085

Printed in the United States of America
10 9 8 7 6 5 4 3 2 1

ISBN 0-87406-386-8

One

HE'LL be there this time, I told myself. *Stop worrying, Darcy Gallatin.* I was staring out the bus window. I didn't feel like talking to anyone. We were on the main highway to Everett, where my dad was supposed to pick us up. At least, Mom said he would when I called last night from Pullman.

"What did you think of Washington State University?" Lynn asked, breaking into my thoughts. I remembered the red brick buildings and the small town clustered around the college. I had been a little scared at first, but everyone was so nice and friendly. I was more sure than ever that I wanted to go to college there after I graduated from high school. Graduation was still five years away, though. It seemed like a long, long time.

"Umm, I really liked it," I answered. "Your aunt and uncle are so nice."

Lynn gave me a searching look. "Are your parents still fighting?" she asked.

"Dad gets drunk, and Mom yells," I answered with a shrug. I looked through the dusty window at the highway. Lynn's question made me think about how different my family is from her aunt and uncle. Spending three weeks with Lynn's relatives had been so peaceful. Lynn's been my best friend for about three years. She knows some stuff about my dad, but not everything. I just haven't been able to tell her everything.

"Do you want to talk to my dad about it?" Lynn offered.

"Oh, I don't want him to know," I answered. Lynn's dad, Dr. Fred, is the town veterinarian. I think he's just about the greatest. The reason I want to go to Washington State is that they have a good veterinary school. I try to get good grades so I can have a veterinary practice like Dr. Fred's. It's hard to get into veterinary school, but I'm going to make it.

Everyone in Stilly Falls calls Lynn's dad Dr. Fred. It's a lot nicer than what they call my dad. He's Roaring Rory Gallatin. He's a logger, and loggers can be pretty rowdy. My dad says he's the biggest, meanest, and loudest of all.

"Everett!" the bus driver called.

I looked out the window. I didn't see my dad's battered, red pickup.

"Where do you suppose your dad is?" Lynn asked as we climbed down the steps of the bus.

"He'll be here," I said, hoping I was right.

"Why don't you call to make sure he's on his way?" Lynn said.

"Okay," I said, heading for the phone.

I dialed my number and my younger brother answered. "Mitch, this is Darcy. We're in Everett. Where's Dad?"

"I don't know. He said something about stopping by Dave's place," Mitch explained.

I glared at the phone. I knew what that meant. Dave and my dad have been buddies since they were kids. They probably got busy doing something, and Dad forgot all about me.

"Call there, and tell him we're waiting. Okay?" I asked.

"Sure. What's your number? I'll call you right back," Mitch answered.

Mitch has a good head on his shoulders, although he flunked fifth grade. He seems to have a hard time concentrating on schoolwork. I try to help him as much as I can. Mom does too. She's a teacher. Together we're going to help Mitch pass this year.

"What happened?" Lynn asked after I hung

up. "Is he coming to pick us up?"

I shrugged. "He told Mitch that he might stop at a friend's house on the way here. Mitch is going to see if he's still there. He's probably just running a little late," I lied. I couldn't tell Lynn we might not even have a ride home. I was used to being left places. I felt bad that Lynn had to put up with it, too.

"He'll probably be here any minute," Lynn decided. "I'm going to get our stuff."

"I'll wait for Mitch to call," I said.

Lynn disappeared inside the bus station. I could tell she was a little irritated.

I waited, wishing Dr. Fred had been the one to pick us up. He would never forget us.

The phone in the phone booth rang, and I picked it up. "Hello, Mitch?"

"Darcy, Dad isn't at Dave's. Mom's teaching summer school, so she can't come get you for hours. I called all the taverns, too, and nobody's seen Dad," Mitch explained.

"He could be on his way here," I said, hoping it was true.

"I'm going to ride my bike around town and see if I can find him. I'll be home in an hour."

"Thanks, Mitch." Like all brothers, Mitch could be a pain sometimes. But it was really great of him to run all over town looking for Dad. I wished I'd gotten him a better present than just a Washington State T-shirt.

"What's up?" Lynn asked, coming out with our stuff.

"I think you'd better call your dad," I suggested.

"Uh-oh, Darcy. He'll be mad about this," Lynn warned. "The last time this happened, he yelled at your dad. You almost didn't get to help at the clinic anymore."

"I'll still help at the clinic," I said firmly. Nothing could keep me from helping out at the clinic.

Lynn dialed the number of her dad's veterinary hospital. The receptionist said he was out on an emergency call.

"Well, let's take the county bus," I suggested.

"I'm ready," Lynn grabbed her suitcase roughly and walked away.

"I'll call Mitch and tell him," I said in a little voice.

"And tell the manager, in case your dad shows up after we leave!" Lynn shouted at me.

When I caught up with Lynn, she was standing on the curb reading the bus schedule. The next bus came in 20 minutes.

"I'm sorry about my dad," I finally said.

Lynn sighed. "lt's okay, Darcy. It's not your fault."

The hour bus ride to Stilly Falls was pretty quiet. I was embarrassed and angry that my dad forgot us. I think Lynn was still a little mad, too.

"Now what?" Lynn snapped, as we got off the bus at the mall on the far edge of town.

"What do you think?" I shot back. "We walk."

Lynn and I glared at each other. We started to walk, both of us in an angry cloud. Then we both saw our reflections in a store window. We were hot, sweaty, and raggedy-looking. We looked so grumpy that I just had to laugh. Then Lynn started to giggle, and I knew everything was all right again.

"Hey, Darcy!"

I turned around and saw Scott Taylor. Scott's been my friend since second grade. We used to catch frogs together in the creek behind our barn. Scott and I used to be able to share everything. But lately, he's just seemed a little childish to me. I mean, he still wants to do the goofy stuff that we did when we were kids. I have more important things to worry about—like veterinary school, my dad, and my horse. Scott just doesn't seem to understand that. I turned my back and kept walking.

"Hey, Darcy! What's going on? It's Scott.

Scott Taylor. Remember me?"

I turned around and saw Scott grinning his ridiculous grin and shook my head. It's not that Scott isn't good-looking. He is. Most of the girls think he's the greatest guy in the whole school. I think he'd be all right, but he does such goofy things—like tease me about catching frogs in front of everyone in science class.

"Come on," Lynn said, catching my arm. "He's not so bad."

"Yeah, you're right," I shot back. "He's worse than bad."

Scott stopped a couple of feet away. I felt pretty awful when I realized he'd heard me.

"Why are you walking? Where are you going?" Scott asked, ignoring my nasty comment.

When I didn't answer, Lynn did. "We're going home. We have to walk because my dad had an emergency, and Darcy's dad got busy."

Scott took Lynn's suitcase and my backpack. He started off across the parking lot. "Come on. My mom will give you a ride home," he said.

"Let's go," Lynn whispered.

I kicked at a rock. "What choice do we have?"

Scott's mother smiled at Lynn and me.

"Welcome home, girls. How was your trip?"

"It was great," Lynn beamed. "We went to lots of classes. We went shopping and to the movies. And Aunt Sophy took us swimming."

Lynn chattered about our visit all the way to Stilly Falls. I was glad that I didn't have to make conversation with Scott. He sat beside me in the backseat. Neither one of us said very much.

We dropped Lynn off first, and she wiggled her little finger. That's our secret signal that means I'm supposed to call her.

"So, did you have fun, Darcy?" Mrs. Taylor asked.

"Yes, ma'am," I answered.

"What happened? Why didn't you girls have a ride home? Your dad is so protective, and so is Dr. Fred."

"Oh," I said, "I guess we just got our signals crossed." I didn't want everyone to know about my dad goofing up and not coming to get us.

"It was a failure to communicate, Mom," Scott interrupted.

"Don't be smart, Scott," Mrs. Taylor said angrily.

I felt a little sorry for Scott. I mean, it's kind of embarrassing for a person to get yelled at in front of another kid.

We stopped at my house, and I jumped out, picking up my backpack. "Thanks, Mrs. Taylor. Bye, Scott."

"I'll come by later," Scott promised. "You'll need help taking care of all your animals."

"I'd rather do it myself," I said.

Scott held the door open. "Oh, no," he said, "I insist."

What could I do? I thanked his mom again and stomped toward my house. Our dogs got up off the front porch and ran barking to meet me. I petted the little one, Winner, and I hugged old Lad. Lad licked my face and kept whining, so I knew he was glad I was home. So was I.

I opened the door, and the dogs and I went inside. Mom came out of the kitchen. "Hi!" I shouted. "I'm home!"

"Darcy!" Mom grabbed me and hugged me for a long time. "I never knew three weeks could be such a long time. Did your dad come get you? Mitch said you called," she said.

"We took the bus, and Mrs. Taylor drove us home from the mall," I explained.

"Well, that was nice of her. Dinner's ready. You have time to wash up. I think Mitch fed all the animals," Mom said, setting the table. "He's outside somewhere."

"I'll dump my things in my room," I said.

"I'm absolutely starving!"

We didn't bother to wait for Dad. Mom usually fixes him a plate and puts it in the oven to keep warm until he gets home. We had started to eat when there was a knock at the front door, and Mom got up to answer it. "Hello, Dr. Fred," I heard her say. "We were having dinner. Come, and join us."

I went into the living room. Dr. Fred looked mad. His jaw looked tight, and his eyes were angry.

"Is something wrong at the clinic?" I asked.

"No, Darcy," he answered, "I came to see your dad. Where is he, Beth?"

Mom was calm, as usual. "He's working with one of the firewood cutters. He isn't home yet," she explained.

"Oh, come on, Beth," said Dr. Fred sharply. He looked at me and added, "Go eat your supper, Darcy. Let me talk to your mom."

I went back in the dining room, but I could still hear Dr. Fred. He was mad because Lynn and I had to find our own way home. Mom kept saying that Dad was working, but I knew she was lying for Dad. I bet Dr. Fred did, too.

Then I heard the front door slam against the wall. I ran out to see what it was, knowing in my heart what I would see. But I wasn't

16

prepared for it to be as bad as it was. Dad stumbled in and fell onto the couch. I had seen him when he'd been drinking before, but I'd never seen him look like that.

His plaid shirt was all rumpled, and one of his suspenders was broken. He hadn't shaved, and his brown hair was a real mess. He was laughing as he tried to push himself back up from the couch. Then he looked around at all of us staring at him. He stopped laughing and pushed himself back up onto his feet.

I just stood there, embarrassed half to death in front of Dr. Fred. "Dad, are you okay?" I asked.

"He's fine," Mom snapped at me. "He's been working, and he's exhausted."

Dad looked from Dr. Fred to me to Mom. "That's right, Fred," he said. "I'm exhausted from a long day of work in the woods." Then he started laughing again. "Nobody can say that Roaring Rory Gallatin isn't the hardest working logger in the state of Washington!" he shouted.

Two

WE all just stood there staring at each other for what seemed like a long time. Then Dr. Fred gave my dad a strange look and said quietly, "I want to talk to you about forgetting to pick up the girls in Everett. I'll come back when you're sober, Rory."

Dad laughed again. What did he think was so funny? "Ah, give me a break, Fred," he said.

Dr. Fred looked at Dad a little bit longer in that same, strange way. Then he said, "Grow up, Rory." He turned around and walked out without shutting the door.

Mom frowned. "I never have liked him. He thinks he's better than everybody else," she said. Then Mom added, "I don't want you working at the clinic, anymore, Darcy. Who does Fred Jensen think he is to come in here and insult us?"

"What insult?" I asked. "Dad didn't come get us. We had to take the bus home. Dr. Fred was worried about us."

"It was broad daylight for heaven's sake," Mom said.

"Leave the kid alone, Beth," Dad ordered. Then they started arguing about why Dad didn't come pick us up and if I could still work at the clinic.

I ran outside to the barn. Had I only been away for three weeks? It seemed like all these people were strangers. Mitch kept right on eating, like he was watching a TV show about some family arguing. He didn't seem to react at all.

At times like this, I find myself thinking what things would be like if my family was more like Lynn's. Even though Lynn's mom had left them years ago, and even though Lynn and Dr. Fred are terrible cooks and eat supper at the cafe in town half the time, they seem to really care about each other. They look out for each other. It's just the two of them.

I walked by the doghouses and noticed their water dishes were empty. *Darn that Mitch,* I thought. *He was supposed to look after these guys.* Then I turned the corner and saw my horse.

Brandy was lying down. My eyes filled up with tears. She was covered with mud, straw, and muck. The stall was filthy. It obviously hadn't been cleaned the entire time I was gone. Dad had promised he would take good care of my horse. Was this what he called good care?

At least there was hay in her manger. But Brandy's sides were caved in, and I guessed that she hadn't had any water today. It was so hot. What was Dad thinking? If he and I didn't take care of the animals, it didn't get done. And I hadn't been here to do it.

I took a deep breath. *Oh well, I'm here now. First things first,* I told myself. I put a halter on Brandy and led her outside to the creek. She tanked up on water. Once she finished drinking, I tied her to a post and went to check the fences.

We have five acres of land. That's not a whole lot, but it's nice to have some space to ride my horse. We're close to town. Actually, Stilly Falls is so small that everything is close to town. Stilly Falls only has two paved streets. The rest of the streets are gravel.

The fences were okay, so I turned Brandy out into the pasture. She took off running and bucking. At first she was a little bit stiff, so I knew she'd been locked up for longer than a day. Finally, she got down and began to roll. I was glad. Maybe some of the crud would come off, and it would be easier to brush her. I headed for the barn. Now I had to muck her stall. It's not my favorite job, but a horse needs a clean place to live, doesn't she?

I should have changed into my old jeans, but why bother? I wondered. I didn't want to hear Mom and Dad arguing. Besides, if I went into the house and saw my younger brother, I'd want to punch him. Then I'd be grounded past forever. I got the wheelbarrow and manure fork, and I began pitching.

Being angry about the way Dad and Mitch had forgotten to look after Brandy made the job go fast. The sun had already set when I finished. I noticed that the barn loft was empty. I had to tell Dad to get some more hay tomorrow. Considering the shape he was in, I wondered if he'd remember.

Mom met me on the back porch. "Darcy, where have you been?" she asked.

"Mucking Brandy's stall," I answered. "Where's Dad? I want to ask him to get some more hay tomorrow."

Mom just frowned and said Dad had gone out.

I knew where Dad probably was. I also knew

22

that the bars closed at 2 a.m., and I wanted to stay up until then. I told Mom I wanted to watch the late movie. But I couldn't stay awake. I woke up when Dad touched my shoulder. "Hi," I said sleepily.

"Hi, yourself," Dad said in his big, deep voice. "What are you doing out here? You should be in bed, Darcy."

"I was watching the movie," I said rubbing my eyes. The room looked silvery-gray as the sign-off pattern glowed from the TV screen. "I guess I must have fallen asleep."

"It couldn't have been the greatest movie in the world," Dad chuckled. "Are you mad at me, honey?"

"No," I replied honestly. "It never does any good."

Dad sat down beside me, and I could smell the booze on his breath. "I got work today, and I forgot to come get you and Lynn. I'll bet Fred still wants to hang me out to dry."

I snuggled close and felt the thick cotton of Dad's flannel shirt against my cheek. It was like when he used to hold me when I was a little kid.

"Dad, why didn't Brandy's stall get cleaned?" I asked.

Dad stroked my hair. "Because your old man messed up, baby. I know Mitch is afraid

23

of horses. I just forgot to check on Brandy. It's my fault."

"Dad," I said after awhile. "We're almost out of hay."

"Do we have enough for morning chores?" Dad asked.

"Probably," I guessed.

Dad stood up and pulled me to my feet. "I'll bring in a load first thing in the morning."

"Okay," I said with a yawn.

Dad hugged me. "I'm glad you're home," he said with a smile.

I went up to my room and crawled into bed, but I couldn't fall asleep right away. The moon was bright, and it shone through the window. Our furry, gray cat, Happy, purred next to me. All kinds of thoughts were jumping around in my head.

I knew it was wrong to wish that my dad was more like Dr. Fred, but I couldn't help it sometimes. *What did that strange look that Dr. Fred gave my dad mean? When is Mitch going to wake up? I mean, sometimes he's like a person who's walking in his sleep. And how much longer can Mom keep trying to protect Dad?* I remembered how she told Dr. Fred that Dad was just tired when she knew that wasn't true.

The last thing I saw before I finally fell asleep was the moonlight shining in through the window onto my bag of presents for the family. I hadn't even had time to pass them out. Nobody even asked if I brought them anything.

Three

THE next morning, Dad slept while we all got ready to go to church, and he slept the whole time we were gone. When we got home, I called the feed store. They were open, and there was plenty of hay.

I filled a cup with coffee and went to wake Dad. "It's afternoon, and you promised to haul hay," I said.

Dad groaned and reached for the cup. "Can't that horse eat grass?"

"Dad, you know that she can't," I groaned. "Dr. Fred says there isn't enough nutrition in our grass."

"That darned horse eats better than I do," Dad grumped. "Get out, so I can get dressed, girl. Then I'll go buy a ton of your rotten hay."

I couldn't help grinning. For once, he sounded almost like himself. I heard the phone ringing and ran to get it. I heard Lynn's excited voice.

"Darcy, Dad has an emergency! A horse has a cut artery at the riding stable, and we can both go help. Hurry!"

I thought about what Mom had said last night. I wondered if I should go against her words. Dad stuck his head around the corner of the door. "Dr. Fred has an emergency," I told him.

Dad stared at me. "Then what are you doing standing around? I'll get the hay. Move your feet."

"What about Mom?"

"I'll tell her," Dad retorted. "Go."

"Thanks, Dad!" I shouted. I turned back to the phone.

"I'll meet you at the corner." I ran out the door and across the lawn to the road, and I kept running toward the corner.

It didn't take long to drive to the stable. Mrs. Craig waved to us from where she was holding a big, red mare. "What took you so long?"

"We came as fast as we could," Lynn answered.

"I know you did," Mrs. Craig said, and I realized that she was crying. When she lifted away the bandage, I forgot all about everything other than the wound. I was too busy trying not to get sick right there.

This horse had one of the worst cuts I had ever seen. Torn flesh and blood were everywhere. Lynn was turning green. She walked a few steps away and then broke into a run. I heard her being sick over in the bushes.

After a while, Lynn came back. "I'll hold the horse," she told me. "You help Dad."

I gave the rope to Lynn. After a while, I saw that she was beginning to look human again. We cleaned the injury and sewed the leg back together. Lucky for us and the horse, it was a vein that was cut, instead of an artery. Arteries are bigger than veins, and they lead from the heart, full of fresh blood.

After we bandaged and taped the leg from the knee to the hoof, Mrs. Craig slowly led the mare, Sedita, to her stall. Sedita would have to be kept inside for weeks while her leg healed. If any infection started, we'd be in real trouble.

"Would you like something to drink?" Mrs. Craig asked when she came back. She unsnapped a ring of keys from a loop on her jeans. "There are cold soft drinks in the machine."

"Great," Lynn and I answered.

"What about you, Fred?" Mrs. Craig asked. "I'm going to have a beer."

My dad wouldn't have passed up a cold

beer on a hot day, but Dr. Fred was shaking his head. "I'll have a soft drink, too, thanks."

"Are you sure about that beer, Fred? Beer's more nutritious than a soft drink." Mrs. Craig seemed to be teasing him.

Dr. Fred shrugged. "You know I don't drink, Evelyn."

They looked at each other for a long time, and then Mrs. Craig smiled. Dr. Fred grinned back at her. "There's no telling what kind of emergency could be waiting for me back at the office," he said.

While we were packing up Dr. Fred's things, I was thinking about how he had turned down the beer. I just couldn't imagine my dad doing that. Of course, my dad is a logger, and he says that all of the loggers drink a lot. Mom says it's because they work so hard out in the woods and they sweat a lot. She says that they have to replace the liquid in their systems. But water is liquid, and so are soft drinks. I thought about Mrs. Craig's having only *one* beer. I wondered why my dad couldn't drink just one beer, instead of drinking six or eight.

"Hey, Darce, you're in dreamland," Lynn said, poking my arm. "Let's go see the baby pigs in the barn."

"Does Dr. Fred really not drink?" I asked

Lynn when we were alone.

Lynn stared at me. "He never has, not as long as I can remember. Even when Mom left us, he says he just worked harder at the clinic."

I thought about what Lynn had said for the rest of the afternoon. When I got home, Dad and his friend, Dave Stark, were working on Dave's car. Actually, Dad was working, and Dave was watching Dad work. Mitch was passing Dad tools and sorting out long, black wires that looked like licorice. Dave's a logger, too. Mom claims that Dave leads Dad into trouble. But I don't think that's right. After all, Dad's not a little boy. He does what he wants to, and he doesn't let Dave lead him around. I stopped for a minute to say hi, and then I asked, "Did you get the hay, Dad?"

Dad lifted his head and almost cracked it on the hood. "Don't scare me like that, Darcy. Get me a beer. I'll bring in the hay after I finish connecting these plug wires."

How about a soft drink? I felt like asking, but I didn't.

"Bring Dave a beer, too," Dad added.

"Don't bother, little girl. I've got something a lot better," Dave said, and he held up a glass jar of what looked like water.

Only I knew it wasn't water. It was the local

moonshine. Dave buys it from some old guy who lives out in the woods.

"You'll pickle your brain in that stuff, Dave. If that poison doesn't blind you, it'll rot your insides," my dad said.

"It's no wonder you don't like it, Rory. It's a drink for real men." Then Dave held out the jar to my brother. "What about you, boy? Do you want a drink?" Mitch stared at the jar for a while and then turned away.

Dad grabbed Dave's arm and almost made him drop the jar.

Dad looked really mean. His jaw jutted forward, and his eyes were like chips of rock. "What do you think you're doing?" he demanded. "My kids don't drink."

Was this how my dad looked when he got in a fight? I wondered.

Dave backed up a step, laughing nervously. "Hey, come on, Rory. You know I was only joking. You and I were boozing it up when we were their age." He actually looked a little scared.

"I've done a lot of things that I don't want my kids to do," Dad said quietly.

Then Dave said, "Besides, I'm sure they've tasted booze before."

Dad dropped the wrench, and it bounced off the car with a bang and fell into the dirt.

32

"Look, Dave, old buddy. I told you that my kids don't drink. I wouldn't want to be in your shoes if you don't knock it off."

"Take it easy, Rory. Don't get all excited. I was only kidding. I'm sorry." Dave looked really nervous.

Dad went back to working on the car, and I went inside to get his beer. I brought one out for Dave, too.

When I gave Dave his beer, he smiled at me. He made me sick. "How'd you do in school, kid?" Dave asked me. "I'll bet you got straight *A*'s again, huh?"

"Yeah, I did," I answered, with a tone that said, *I don't want to talk to you.*

Dad must have understood that I was upset, because he said, "Go help your mom fix supper, honey."

I started to walk away, and behind me, I heard Dave giving Dad a hard time. Inside, I found Mom lying on her bed, reading the new, fifth-grade history book. So, I went to my room and got out my sewing basket.

I was doing some needlework for Mom's birthday next winter. But when I looked at all the different colors of threads in my hand, all I could see was Sedita's bloody, torn leg. Tears ran down my cheeks and splotched the yellow cloth, but I didn't care. Suddenly, there was a knock at the door.

"Darce, are you all right?" Mitch called. Then he opened the door and came in. He sat down on the bed next to me.

I started to cry harder. I wasn't even sure why I was crying. I didn't know whether I was crying for Mrs. Craig's injured horse, or because Dad's drinking seemed to be getting worse and worse.

I tried to tell Mitch what I was feeling, "Mitch, I feel awful that Dad drinks so much and then gets into trouble because he's drunk," I said.

He just listened, without saying anything. But I could tell that he felt the same way I did. I'm not sure how much time had passed when Mom came into the room. Mitch patted my shoulder and then left quietly.

Mom sat down and put her arm around me. She stroked my hair. "Darcy, what's wrong?" she asked.

I wiped away my tears with the back of my hand. I didn't know what to say to her. I didn't know how I could explain to her what was wrong when I didn't know myself.

"I don't know what's wrong, Mom. I was going to do some sewing, and I just started crying." I sniffled.

Mom hugged me. "Darcy, why don't you

stop sewing for now. Forget about it, and go ride your horse. All you've done since school let out is work. First you were picking berries. Then you were helping the veterinary clinic. Then you went to Pullman and audited those classes. Take a break, Darcy. You're working too hard. This is summer vacation. Life is supposed to be fun, too," Mom said gently.

I hesitated. "Maybe you're right," I said.

Mom sighed. "Why don't you ride to the store, and bring back some oatmeal. We'll make cookies."

"Well, okay," I sniffed and hugged her back. "I guess Dad could take some for his lunches."

When Mom stood up to leave, I felt I had to say something. "Mom, what are we going to do?" I blurted out.

Mom looked at me in a strange way for a moment. Then she said, "What are we going to do about what, Darcy?" Her face became blank.

"Well," I hesitated, "umm, about Dad and us. You know...."

I could tell Mom didn't want to talk about it. She finally looked at me and just said, "We'll keep doing what we've always done. We'll get by, like we always have." Then she left.

Why won't anybody talk to me about this?
I wondered. *What's going to happen?*

Mom was right about one thing, anyway.
Getting out and riding Brandy did make me
feel better. Brandy needed the exercise, too.

After I got back from the store, I started
to make the cookies. I was stirring the peanut
butter and watching it melt into the choco-
late when the back door opened, and Dad
came in. He was carrying a big bouquet of
long-stemmed, red roses.

Mom was tearing off sheets of wax paper
when she looked up and said, "Rory Gallatin,
I'm furious with you." She stopped when she
saw the flowers. "What are those for?" she
asked.

"They're my way of saying I'm sorry," Dad
said. He winked at me. Mom smiled at Dad,
even though she was still mad at him. I
realized that they must love each other in
spite of the way they argued. *But love doesn't
always make things better,* I thought.

Four

FOR the rest of the summer, everything was pretty calm at home. Mom didn't yell at Dad so much, but everybody was still walking on eggshells. Mitch seemed to disappear into the woods for hours every day. And Dad didn't stop drinking. Twice the police chief drove him home after the taverns had closed.

I was glad when school started. On the first day, Lynn met me at the corner, and we walked to school together. When we picked up our schedules, I stared at mine. "Oh, no," I groaned, "I've got Mrs. Wheeler for homeroom *and* for English." Mrs. Wheeler had a reputation for being hard and strict. *Oh, well,* I thought, *I might as well get used to having hard teachers. All the teachers at Washington State will be hard.*

"When do you have lunch?" I asked Lynn. "I have it during the first lunch period," Lynn answered. "How about you?"

"I have it during the first one, too. I'll meet you in the cafeteria at lunch." I hurried down the hall and up the flight of stairs to the third floor. The last bell rang as I ran into the classroom.

Mrs. Wheeler frowned at me. "If you're tardy after this, you'll have to get a pass from the office."

I bit my tongue, so I wouldn't argue with her. Some kids can afford to fight with a teacher. I can't. I just have to get good grades. I sat down in an empty chair.

Mrs. Wheeler shut the classroom door and began to take attendance. When she got to my name, she asked, "Are you Rory Gallatin's daughter?"

I hated that question. Everybody knows my dad, and they all look at me funny because I'm his daughter. "Yes, ma'am," I said, trying hard to be polite.

Mrs. Wheeler looked at me from behind her wire-rimmed glasses and said, "Your dad was one of my best students when he was your age. I hope you're going to work as hard as he did."

I was pretty shocked by her comment, and I knew the rest of the class must have been, too. This wasn't what I was used to hearing about Roaring Rory. *If my dad is so smart,*

I thought, *why does he drink and hang around with Dave Stark?*

Not much happened the rest of the morning, unless you count getting assigned a 2000-word essay by Mrs. Wheeler on the first day of school something. I told Lynn about the essay during lunch, and she couldn't believe it. It was nice to see all of my old friends again after summer vacation. Listening to them talk about what they'd done over vacation helped take my mind off *my* summer.

Scott came over and sat down. Somebody was talking about how they were going to have to dissect frogs in science class. And Scott started blabbing about how I was so scared to touch a frog that I started crying when we were catching frogs back in the second or third grade.

When school let out that afternoon, Mitch was waiting for us on the main steps. "Hey, Mitch," Lynn said, "how'd the first day of school go?"

"It went okay," he answered. "I think I'll pass this time."

Just as we were leaving the school grounds, Scott came running up. "Where are you guys going?" he asked.

"We're going to the veterinary clinic," Lynn told him.

"And we're kind of in a hurry," I added.

"So, I'll walk fast," he said, laughing.

We took turns telling each other all about our classes and teachers. The weather was really beautiful after the long, hot summer. The sky was as blue as a mountain lake, and the leaves on the trees were just starting to turn colors. In spite of everything, I was starting to feel the way fall always makes me feel—happy, excited, and ready to start new things. *Even Scott couldn't put me in a bad mood on a day like this!* I thought.

We were at the alley, past the grocery store and almost to the clinic, when the door of the tavern opened, and a man came out. It was my dad. I could tell he'd been drinking by the way he was walking. I didn't want Lynn or Scott to see him like that, so I just kept walking. Lynn knew that Dad drank, but I didn't think she knew how much he drank. I didn't know what to do.

Then I saw a police car stop right beside Dad. I guessed that Chief Johnson was going to drive Dad home again, like he had done a lot of times before.

Five

I didn't know what to do. I almost went over to the police car to tell Chief Johnson that I'd make sure Dad got home all right. But something stopped me. I just didn't want Lynn and Scott to see Dad this way.

Down the alley, the back door of the clinic was open. I started to run down the alley to the open door. "Come on, Lynn!" I shouted, hoping that she would follow me. "Let's see what's going on." I waved good-bye to Mitch and Scott. Luckily, Lynn flew down the alley with me, and she never saw Dad get into the patrol car. I saw Mitch pointing to a store window, trying to get Scott to look the other way from the police car with Dad in it.

"Hurry up, girls," said Dr. Fred when we went into the clinic. "We got in a hit and run." He was holding a little dog that had been hit by a truck.

* * * * *

I didn't get home until after six that night.
I had tons of homework. Mom was washing the
dinner dishes when I got home. "Aren't you
supposed to be home at 5:00?" she asked with
irritation.

"We had an emergency at the clinic." I put
my books down on the table. "A dog was hit
by a truck, and we saved him."

Mom nodded. "Your dinner's in the oven.
Mitch is at the library."

I was wondering how to explain to Dad
about this afternoon when I pretended not to
see him. But he wasn't home yet.

After I finished my dinner, I helped Mom
clean up, and then I started to do my
homework. If I do my homework at the kitchen
table, sometimes Mom helps me.

Mom had been helping me with my algebra for about a half-hour. "Hmm," she said,
looking at the clock. "It's getting late. I wonder
where your dad is. He said he'd be home for
dinner, and he would have called if he knew
he'd be this late."

I stared at the stack of papers and books
in front of me. Then I took a deep breath
and said, "I saw him on my way to the clinic.

He was talking to Chief Johnson."

Mom looked even more worried. "I'd better call and see if something happened. I'll go into the other room, so I won't bother you."

After a few minutes, Mom came out. Her eyes were red, and her hands were shaking.

"What's wrong? Where's Dad?" I asked.

Mom took a deep breath, but her voice still sounded weak.

"He's in Everett," she said. "I'm going to go get him. Will you go to the library and walk home with Mitch? I want both of you in bed at 9:00."

She hurried out the front door, and I went after her. "What's happened to Dad?"

Mom opened the door of her old Mustang. "He's in jail. He was arrested because he didn't leave the bar fast enough to suit the new bartender at the Cross-Cut Tavern."

"It's my fault that he's in Everett, Mom," I said, starting to cry. "I saw him with Chief Johnson. I should have gone over to him, but I didn't want Lynn and Scott to see Dad like that."

Mom smoothed my hair and then hugged me. "We have to take care of your dad, Darcy. We can't run away from our responsibilities."

I watched Mom drive away. I felt like the whole thing was my fault. I never should have pretended not to see Dad. I should have gone over and tried to explain the situation to Chief Johnson, so that he would let me take Dad home. I decided that it was my responsibility to accept that I have a father who drinks a lot. *It's just what I have to do,* I thought.

Later that night, I lay there in the dark, listening for Mom's car. But I fell asleep before Mom and Dad got home. Happy lay on my feet, purring. I sat up and pulled Happy into my arms. I held him for a long time with my eyes closed. When I looked at my alarm clock, it was 11:15. I closed my eyes and tried to sleep.

I woke up when I heard somebody pounding on the front door. It was 4:10. *Did Mom and Dad come home at all?* I wondered.

I got up and put on my robe. I crept downstairs to see who was pounding on the door. I could see Mom at the front door, talking to a man I couldn't see. For a moment, I thought that this man might be telling Mom that something terrible had happened to Dad.

But then I heard Mom's tired voice say, "Rory won't be going to work today. He has the flu."

It was one of the men in the the car pool that came early every morning to take Dad to work.

What was going on? Was Dad home? Was he sick?

"Darcy, what are you doing up?" Mom asked when she saw me.

"I heard the knocking, and I was going to answer the door. Is Dad home?" I asked.

Mom patted my shoulder. "He's upstairs." she said. "He just needs to get some sleep."

I yawned and looked at my books. "Well, since I'm up, I guess I'll finish my homework." I still had to write Mrs. Wheeler's essay.

By the time I finished my homework, it was time to get dressed and go to the barn. I had barely enough time to do the chores, take a shower, eat, get dressed, and hurry to meet Lynn. My eyes burned, and I felt really tired. I wondered how I'd ever make it through the day.

Lynn met me on the corner, like she always did. "The dog's doing great. He managed to drink a little water," she said. It took me a while to realize that she was talking about the dog that was brought into the clinic yesterday.

"That's great." I tried to sound excited, but I could hear my voice dragging.

"Are you okay, Darce?" Lynn asked, looking at me.

"I'm just tired." I could tell Lynn was staring

at me as we walked along. I just couldn't get up the energy to say anything.

Finally, she said, "Look, Darcy, are we best friends, or not? If there's something bothering you, then you should tell me about it. That's all I'm going to say!"

We walked on a little farther. I finally decided that I had to tell someone how I felt about my father's drinking problem. Lynn *was* my best friend, and best friends *are* there for you to tell things to.

I took a deep breath to feel calmer. "Remember when we were going to the clinic, and I made you go down the alley? That was because Dad was outside the tavern with Chief Johnson. He was getting arrested for fighting, or for being drunk or something. I didn't want you to see him like that. My dad's so different from your dad. I feel rotten because I should have gone over there, instead of being ashamed and trying to sneak away."

The words came tumbling out of me. "And, Lynn," I added, "that isn't the first time he's acted that way. My dad's been arrested lots of times before for being drunk."

We were almost to the school when Lynn stopped and asked softly, "Darcy, what would you have done? Even if you had gone over to your dad, do you really think that Chief

Johnson wouldn't have arrested him? You're just a kid, Darcy. There's only so much you can do."

"Maybe you're right, Lynn, but I can't help feeling responsible," I said. "He *is* my dad. My mom says that we have to look out for him."

Just then, the first bell rang, and Lynn and I had to run to our classrooms. I plopped into my seat in Mrs. Wheeler's homeroom just before the second bell rang. When her English class started, the first thing Mrs. Wheeler did was take attendance. Then she collected our homework. After that, she started lecturing about the proper sentence and paragraph structure.

My eyelids got heavier and heavier. I was just like a little kid, trying to stay awake to wait for Santa Claus. By the middle of the second period, I was trying everything to stay awake. I pinched myself. I bit my tongue. I sat straight up in my seat. My head started to droop. Mrs. Wheeler started talking about adverbs and adjectives, and that's the last thing I remember.

The *next* thing I remember is my dad standing over my desk, calling my name. I pushed myself up and opened my eyes. He was right there in my English class. He hadn't shaved, and I could smell whiskey on his breath.

"What are you doing here?" I asked and glanced quickly around the room. Everybody was staring at us.

Mrs. Wheeler said, "You fell asleep, Darcy. I thought that someone should come and get you, so I called your dad."

If only she had woken me up instead of calling Dad. He was wearing his oldest jeans, a scuzzy shirt, and his logging boots. I don't think he'd even combed his hair. And everyone had seen my dad this way. I wanted to crawl under a rock.

Dad put his arm around me. "Come on, honey. I'll take you to the doctor. Then we can go home."

"But I'm okay. Can't I stay? I was just–" My voice stopped. I looked around at everyone staring at me. I decided that I had to get out of there. I got my books and left. Dad kept his arm around me, but I think it was mostly because he needed help walking.

"I bet Mom will yell at me about this," I said, fighting back tears.

"No, she won't," answered Dad. "But she *will* yell at me for ending up in jail last night."

Luckily, the halls were empty. But I still said, "Don't talk about it here, Dad. Please?"

Six

THE doctor said I was just tired. I knew that. I fell asleep in class, didn't I? He also said that I had lost eight pounds since my last checkup. He told me that I had to get some rest.

Dad took me home and sent me up to bed. I was determined to stay awake and work on my homework, but I fell asleep, anyway. I guess I was pretty tired.

I woke up when Mom came in. She sat down on the bed and put her hand on my forehead, the way she does when I have a fever. "I'm fine," I told her. "Can I get up?"

"I guess so," Mom said, stroking my hair. "You've been sleeping all afternoon."

"Great. Then I'll get on over to the clinic," I said, hopping up.

"Oh, no, you don't," Dad said, standing in the doorway. "You're staying home and just resting." The tone of Dad's voice told me that it wouldn't do any good to argue.

I was pretty hungry by dinnertime, because I slept through lunch. Mom hurried us through the meal, but she only pushed the food around on her plate.

"Darcy, will you clear the dishes?" she asked. "I'll wash them when I get home."

"Where are you going?" Dad asked.

Mom gave Dad a serious look and said, "I'm going to a meeting at the church with Jackie Wheeler."

Dad wasn't used to Mom going out by herself in the evenings, so he seemed a little surprised. After giving Mitch and me a confused look, he followed Mom out the front door. We heard her car drive away. Then Dad popped his head into the kitchen and said, "I'm going over to Dave's to watch a fight on TV for a while. Darcy, you look after Mitch."

We heard the door slam shut. "I guess he's mad because Mom's going to a meeting," I said.

"What kind of meeting do you suppose it is?" Mitch asked.

"Some kind of teacher thing probably," I answered. "Jackie Wheeler is Mrs. Wheeler, my English teacher."

Mom got home around 10:00. She didn't say

anything about the meeting.

The next morning I was late getting to Mrs. Wheeler's class, and I had to knock and wait for her to answer the door. She took my note and waved me to my seat. Most of the girls smiled at me, and one of the guys gave me a thumbs-up.

I ignored them and concentrated on taking notes. Mrs. Wheeler was still lecturing us on sentence structure. During the first break, I took my schoolwork for the day before up to Mrs. Wheeler's desk. "I'm sorry about falling asleep in class yesterday. I had a really bad night the night before. I thought I would be okay." I shrugged.

Mrs. Wheeler took the papers and began to sort through the assignments. "Is there trouble at home, Darcy?"

How would she know about trouble at home? I wondered.

"No, it's nothing. I just didn't sleep very well. That's all," I said. Well, that was true as far as the reason that I had fallen asleep in class.

"Darcy, if you ever want to talk about anything, I'll be happy to talk to you. Anything that affects your schoolwork is important to me," Mrs. Wheeler said. She smiled at me.

While we were talking, the bell rang. I went back to my seat. I didn't know if it was just my imagination, or if Mrs. Wheeler was being nicer to me throughout the rest of the class.

That evening when I got home from the clinic, Mom was fixing supper, and Dad was glaring at her.

"I'm going out for a drink, Beth!" he said loudly.

"That's nice, dear." Mom glanced at me. "Get washed up, Darcy. Mitch, set the table."

"Did you hear me?" Dad shouted.

"Of course, I did, Rory. You're going out. Are you going out before or after supper?" asked Mom.

Dad stared at her as if she'd come from outer space. Then he went over and sat down at the table. "Uhh, I guess I might as well eat first," he answered.

Mitch and I stared at each other. This was really weird. Mom always got angry and quiet when Dad announced that he was going out drinking. This time it seemed like she wasn't paying any attention to him. It was as if he had said that he was going to read the newspaper or something. *What was going on?*

After dinner, Dad got up. "I'm going uptown for a drink!" he announced in his loudest voice.

Mom kept clearing away the table. "Whatever you want, dear." She looked at Mitch and me. "Get your homework, kids. You can do your math out here, Mitch. And I'll help you. Darcy, are you still having trouble with your algebra?"

"Beth, I'm going to get drunk!" Dad yelled. "What do you think about that?"

"Have a good time, Rory. And don't make too much noise when you get home. The kids need their sleep, and I have to give a history test tomorrow," Mom answered.

Dad was staring at her as if he'd been hit over the head with a log. He stomped to the front door, muttering to himself. We heard the door slam shut as he left. Mom kept cleaning up the kitchen.

Mitch and I worked on our homework together at the kitchen table for a while. Mom was in and out of the kitchen, cleaning up and getting her history test ready for tomorrow. We heard her go upstairs finally, and Mitch and I were alone downstairs.

"What do you think's going on, Darce?" Mitch asked carefully. "Mom's really acting different."

"I know, Mitch. Who knows what she's thinking? The last few months have really been tough for her. Maybe she's trying to change her attitude about Dad's drinking. Maybe any change at all would be for the better," I answered. I was pretty confused, too, though.

Mitch was quiet for a while. He was just staring out into the distance, like he was looking through the walls of our house toward the woods and mountains. Then he whispered, "Darcy, can I ask you something?"

"Sure, Mitch," I said. He sounded so serious. "Are you worried about something?" I whispered, even though I knew that Mom was upstairs, and Dad was out.

"Have you ever had a drink?" he asked.

"Do you mean alcohol?" I asked.

"Yeah."

I got up and shut the kitchen door, so that Mom wouldn't surprise us. "No, Mitch, I haven't. Have you?"

He didn't say anything. He just nodded.

"When? And why? Where did you get it?" I asked, still whispering. It was so quiet that I could hear an owl hooting outside in the trees.

"Last fall, I was out messing around in the woods with some guys, and we found half a bottle of whiskey under a bush. They started to drink out of the bottle. I didn't want to, and the smell was awful. But then they started to call me chicken and other things, so I drank some of it. It really burned my throat, and it made me feel dizzy and sick."

"Oh, Mitch," I said, shaking my head.

"I never wanted to, but I didn't want them to think I wasn't cool. It made me feel like I was one of the guys, like I was a big man. I was afraid to not drink with them. I didn't want them to make fun of me."

I looked Mitch right in the eye. "You won't do it again, will you?" I asked.

"No, Darcy, I won't. I don't want to be like Dad. I want to be like you, and get out of this town. I don't want to be some old logger, and hang around bars. You know that I want to be a pilot."

"If you want to get out of Stilly Falls and be a pilot, then you have to work hard in school, Mitch," I told him. "You can't afford to flunk again."

"I know, Darce. I'm just scared that I'll be like Dad. Do you think I will because I drank that whiskey?"

Mitch looked really frightened. "No, Mitch, I don't think you're going to end up like Dad. I know you won't start drinking." I wanted Mitch to know that I had faith in him. It's really important for people to know that other people have faith in them.

"I want to earn some money, too, so that I can start saving it, like you do," Mitch added after a while.

I thought about the money in my Garfield bank on my shelf. All the money that I make doing chores or odd jobs goes into my bank. I have over $200 in it.

"I'll take you berry-picking next summer. You can start saving your own money then," I said.

"That would be great, Darcy," he said. Then we hugged for a long time.

Lying in my bed that night, I thought about something that Mitch had said. *I didn't want them to think I wasn't cool,* he had said. *It made me feel like I was one of the guys, like I was a big man.* I wondered if that was the reason Dad drinks the way he does? *Does he drink to feel like a big man? Why did the roughest, toughest guy is Stilly Falls have to be drunk to feel like a big man?*

Seven

OVER the next few weeks, I kept wondering about Mom's meetings. Two nights a week, she went to different meetings. She never talked about them at home, but she seemed a lot calmer and nicer to be around since she began going to her meetings. It was as if somebody had taken a big load off her shoulders. I knew that that somebody wasn't Dad.

One crisp, beautiful day in October, I came home from school and saw Dad and Dave working on Dave's car. *That old junker never runs right,* I almost said. Dave was sipping moonshine out of a jar.

I tried to walk behind the barn, so that I wouldn't have to talk to Dave. But he saw me and shouted, "Hey, Darcy, do you want a swallow?" He held the jar out to me.

"No, thanks. I don't drink," I answered coldly.

"You're pushing your luck," Dad muttered to Dave. "Knock it off."

"Go help your mom fix supper, Darcy," Dad said to me. "She's going out tonight."

Dave got a sneaky look on his face and said, "How does she like those Al-Anon meetings that she goes to?"

Dad quit smiling. "Beth doesn't go to those meetings," he said quickly.

"Oh, yes, she does," said Dave, like one little kid teasing another. "I saw her coming out of the church the other night. That's where they meet."

Dad dropped the wrench he was holding onto the ground. He looked like somebody had punched him. He walked right into the house where Mom was cooking.

"What's Al-Anon?" I asked Dave.

Dave laughed. The sound grated on my nerves. "It's a group for the wives of alcoholics. I guess your mom forgot to tell your dad." I hated the sound of Dave's laughing. He took a big drink from his jar.

"I bet all your ex-wives went to Al-Anon!" I yelled at him and ran into the house.

Mom was alone in the kitchen with her back to me. I couldn't see Dad anywhere. Mom didn't turn around or speak. Her shoulders were shaking, and I could hear sobs. I put

58

my arms around her and asked, "Mom, are you okay?"

She kept crying, and I felt scared to see her lose control like that. She's always been so strong, and she never breaks down like that.

"I don't know what to do," Mom sobbed. "Your dad keeps drinking, and I don't know how to stop him. I love him, and I don't want him to die."

"What do you mean? Dad isn't going to die," I said.

"He could, Darcy. He takes too many chances, working in the woods when he's drunk. He drives when he's drunk. He could die in a car wreck."

She went on crying. I wanted to run away and come back when she was herself again, but I knew I couldn't. I had to stay with her. She was my mother. I just stayed there with her until she stopped crying.

I fixed dinner that night, with a little help from Mitch. Mom had been talking on the phone. I had heard her crying and explaining about Dad running out. When Mom sat down to eat, her eyes were red.

"Where's Dad?" asked Mitch.

"He went drinking," Mom said. Then she took a deep breath. "I've got something to tell you," she said. "I've been going to Al-Anon meetings."

Mitch asked, "What's that?"

"It's for the wives of alcoholics," I said to Mitch. Then I asked Mom, "How do you know Dad's an alcoholic? He has a job and a family. He's not a bum. He doesn't look like those street people on the news."

Mitch said, "Well, he sure drinks a lot for somebody who's not an alcoholic."

Mom didn't seem to hear him. "It's been hard for me to accept it, Darcy. But all different kinds of people can be alcoholics. Rich, poor, clean, and dirty people can be alcoholics. At Al-Anon, we talk about what it's like to live with someone who drinks, and about how to have a healthy family. I've done a lot of things with your dad that I'd like to change."

"What about Dad?" Mitch asked. "It doesn't seem like he's trying to change. He's getting worse."

"Mitch, I can't stop your dad from drinking. Nobody can. He has to do it himself," Mom said.

"You used to say that it was our responsibility to look after Dad," I reminded Mom.

She looked down and said, "I know I used to say that, Darcy. I was wrong."

"Grandma said that he started drinking when he was 14 years old," Mitch said.

"That's right," Mom answered. "He dropped out of school to go into the army. Back then, he could drink as soon as he was in uniform. Your dad's been drinking for over 20 years, and I don't know if he can stop."

All the time Mom was talking about Dad being an alcoholic, I could only think of those old men lying in the gutter in big cities. They had filthy clothes and no teeth. They were homeless, and they didn't have families like ours.

"Dad can't be an alcoholic, Mom. He doesn't drink all the time," I said. "He's a logger. They all drink. You said so."

"I was wrong about that, too, Darcy. I've been wrong about a lot of things," Mom said quietly.

Then Mitch added, "Most of the guys in my class have dads who are loggers. They don't drink the way our dad does. Our dad drinks more than anybody else."

"Except Dave Stark," I added.

"I'm worried about you guys, too," said Mom.

"Why? What have we done?" I asked.

"Nothing, Darcy Ann, you haven't done anything at all. I'm scared because the children of alcoholics are much more likely to become alcoholics themselves. I don't want you or Mitch to become an alcoholic."

When Mom said that, I looked at Mitch. He turned white, like he had seen a ghost.

"We don't drink, Mom," Mitch answered firmly. "And we're not going to start." He nodded at me.

Mom looked at the clock and said, "It's late, you two. We've had a long day."

"I think it's good we're talking about this, Mom," I said when we all stood up.

"I agree, Darcy," she answered. "We'll have to do a lot more talking, too." She gave us both a long hug.

As I was going up the stairs, I turned around to look at Mom. She had turned out the light in the kitchen and was sitting, staring out the window. The house was perfectly quiet, except for the sound of her soft crying coming from the kitchen table.

Eight

OVER the next three days, Dad came home only to change clothes and leave for work. The rest of the time, he was off drinking. I didn't even see him once. But when I got home from school on Friday, Dad was sitting at the kitchen table with Mom.

He was staring at his coffee cup like he'd never seen it before. I went to hug Dad. He just sat there like a statue. I was really glad to see him, even though he looked kind of strange. Mitch had come in right after me.

"Sit down, kids. Your dad has something to tell you," Mom said.

Dad looked at both of us and then at his cup.

Mom said, "You have to tell them, Rory. I won't."

Dad didn't say anything.

Finally, Mom said, "Okay, Rory, would you

rather they hear about it at school tomorrow from other loggers' kids? That's fine with me."

"Is that more of your Al-Anon stuff?" Dad grumbled.

"What did you do, Dad?" Mitch asked.

Dad picked up his cup of coffee. "I got fired," he said.

I went over and put my arms around him.

"I've been drinking a lot. I was still drunk when I went to work today. Dave was supposed to be helping my crew. He wanted to fall some trees. I wouldn't let him. Not at first, anyhow. Dave kept after me, and finally, I handed my saw to him and told him to go ahead. He started cutting a small alder that was pulpwood size."

Dad paused and shook his head. "I still don't know how it happened. When the tree fell, it landed on Dave. He was trapped under it, and both of his legs were broken. I had to lift the tree off him."

"Well, why did you get fired?" Mitch asked. "It was Dave's fault."

Dad looked at him. "Yes, son, it was Dave's fault," he said. "But my boss didn't see it that way. He said that I was in charge of the crew and that I was responsible. So, I got fired."

"Can you get your unemployment?" I asked.

Dad shook his head. "Not yet. I have to

wait two months to get it."

"Well, you'll get another job long before then," Mom said. She came over and kissed Dad. "I have faith in you, Rory Gallatin."

Just like I had faith in Mitch when he told me he wouldn't drink anymore, I thought. "I have faith in you, too, Dad," I said.

"I'll look for another job first thing in the morning," Dad promised. "I bet I'll have a new job before you're out of school."

But he didn't get another job. None of the other logging companies would hire him. It didn't matter when Dave tried to clear my dad's name, either. Nobody believed that Dave dropped the tree on his own legs. They all figured that Roaring Rory Gallatin did it.

For the following couple of weeks, Dad was gone more than he was home, between looking for a job and drinking at taverns. I didn't see him much. I was doing homework one night when the phone rang. I answered it, and Chief Johnson asked to talk to Mom.

Mom was calm when she answered the phone. "What can I do for you, Chief?" She listened for a while, and then she said. "No, I won't come down to the jail for him. Rory's a grown man. If he wants to drink, he has to accept the consequences," she said, and then she hung up the phone.

I stared at her. "You're going to let them take Dad to jail after all he's been through? That's not fair!" I shouted.

Mom came over and sat down next to me. "What's not fair, Darcy? Is it fair that we should all have to suffer because Dad drinks and gets into trouble? Your father is an adult. Sooner or later, he has to learn to take care of himself. I can't spend the rest of my life taking care of him. I know he got a bad deal with Dave and the logging companies, but he brought it on himself. He had no business going to work drunk. Maybe spending a night in jail will make him appreciate sleeping at home."

I was practically a wreck in school the next day. Mrs. Wheeler must have noticed, because she asked me to talk to her during the break. I just didn't feel like talking, but she called me over.

"How's your dad doing, Darcy?" she asked. "Is he still drowning his guilt about the accident in the woods in booze?"

"How...how do you know about that?" I asked.

"Your mother told me about it. Darcy, have you ever thought about coming to one of our Alateen meetings? They're for teenagers who are affected by an alcoholic," she said with a kind look. "It might help," she added.

I couldn't stand the thought of her thinking that my dad was a worthless, no-good drunk. I didn't want the whole town knowing our private stuff.

"No, I haven't," I said. "Besides, my dad's not an alcoholic. He's just having a tough time right now. He'll be better when he gets a job."

Mrs. Wheeler looked at me for a while, and then she opened her purse. She took out an old photograph of a man wearing a suit and a hat like an old-time gangster.

"This is my husband, Darcy," Mrs. Wheeler told me. "He was an alcoholic. He died a long time ago in a car accident. I still miss him."

It was almost like she read my thoughts, because then she said, "You know, Darcy, not all alcoholics are dirty, homeless people. My husband always wore a clean shirt and shined shoes. He was a lawyer first and then a judge. A lot of people respected him, but he was still an alcoholic. And he was still hard to live with sometimes."

The other kids started coming back into the classroom. Mrs. Wheeler stood up and said softly, so the others wouldn't hear, "Just think about coming to a meeting, Darcy. It might help."

When I walked into the cafeteria at lunchtime, I saw Lynn saving me a place. I walked over to our regular table, wondering if other kids were staring at me.

"I'm not having a very good day," I told her as I sat down.

"Why? What's up?" Lynn asked.

It felt good to tell Lynn all about what Mom had said last night and what Mrs. Wheeler had said today. Lynn listened to everything I said.

"I hope you won't be mad, Darce, but I think they're right. I think your dad might be an alcoholic. He drinks an awful lot, and I don't know if he could stop," Lynn said.

She probably thought she was saying the right thing, but it sounded like the wrong thing to me then. I didn't need my best friend on my case about my dad being an alcoholic, too. It was bad enough with my English teacher. I lost my cool.

"Lynn, you just don't understand. Stop bugging me about Dad! He's not an alcoholic." I noticed that the kids at the nearby tables were staring at me, so I tried to keep my voice down. "I thought you were my friend!" I hissed. I stood up and walked out of the cafeteria.

I had never skipped school in my life, but

I just couldn't go to class that afternoon. I sneaked out one of the rear doors and headed for the woods on the edge of town. I just had to clear my mind. The air was getting cooler. I could tell that winter was getting closer. Walking through the woods always helped me sort things out. This time, though, everything was too mixed up. I walked and walked, but the questions were still there. I wondered how I would ever find any answers. *Could my dad really be an alcoholic? Were Lynn and I finished as best friends? Could I ever help at the clinic again? Had I blown my chance to go to W.S.U. and to be a veterinarian by skipping school? Were Mitch and I in danger of becoming alcoholics? Should I follow Mrs. Wheeler's advice and go to one of those meetings? Were Mom and Dad headed for divorce?*

I sat down on an old log and pulled my jacket tighter around me. Everything that had happened whirled around in my brain until I couldn't keep it in anymore. I let the tears come.

I must have sat there an hour or more. I noticed that it was starting to get dark. I did feel calmer, though, even if I didn't have any answers. The one thing I did decide was to check out one of those meetings that Mrs.

Wheeler talked about. *It couldn't hurt, could it?* I wondered. I might even get some answers to my questions.

Nine

I didn't tell anyone about skipping school. I couldn't have stayed in school the way I felt, and there are just some things you have to do. I told myself that I'd have to work really hard to make up for skipping school that afternoon.

Walking to the corner the next morning, I was a little afraid that Lynn might not be there to meet me. But I breathed a big sigh of relief when I saw her there, waiting for me. We smiled at each other and started walking.

"I'm really sorry about yesterday," I said to Lynn. "I've just had so many things to worry about lately."

"Hey, Darce," she said, putting her arm around me, "we're best friends. Enough said."

"You're right," I replied. "Well, I guess that's one less thing I have to worry about."

As we walked to school, I told Lynn that I

had decided to go to an Alateen meeting that Mrs. Wheeler had told me about. There was a meeting tonight. Lynn thought, as I did, that it couldn't hurt.

"Who knows?" she added. "Maybe you'll find out for sure if your dad is an alcoholic or not."

Luckily, we had a movie in the auditorium for both English periods. I didn't have to talk to Mrs. Wheeler. I was feeling a little funny about our talk yesterday.

As for skipping class, I went to the school nurse at lunch period and just told her the truth. I said I had felt sick and had to take a walk and get some fresh air. She remembered how Dad had to come and take me home. She must have thought that I was still feeling tired from that. In a way, I guess that was true. She wrote an excuse for me to get back into class and told me to take care of myself.

As I walked into the kitchen after school, I decided I'd tell Mom right away about going to the meeting. I was afraid that if I didn't tell someone, I might chicken out and not go. I told Mom that I was pretty nervous and that I didn't know what to expect at the meeting. She said not to worry about it, and that everyone would be very nice to me.

Dad wasn't home for dinner, as usual. Mom arranged for Mitch to go to the library. It was a nice night, so we walked the few blocks to the church.

Inside the church, Mom introduced me to several people. Mom said that everybody called everyone else by first name. I kind of liked that. That is, until Mrs. Wheeler came up to us, smiling. I couldn't call my English teacher by her first name.

"The Alateen group is downstairs," Mrs. Wheeler said. "Al-Anon is for adult friends or relatives of alcoholics or people with drinking problems. Alateen is for kids your age who are affected by drinking. Come on, I'll go down with you."

That was how I went to my first Alateen meeting. There were about 10 kids in the basement meeting room. I had seen some of them around, but I really didn't know any of them.

The meeting went on for two hours. It started with reading the 12 Steps of Alateen. I learned a lot of things about alcoholism. Mrs. Wheeler spoke for some of the time. She said that alcoholism is a disease. She said that the disease makes people do things they really don't want to do, and that they can't help doing it.

The things Mrs. Wheeler, Jackie, said made me think about my dad. My dad was the biggest, toughest man in Stilly Falls. He could lift a tree off of Dave Stark's legs. But he couldn't keep himself from lifting up a glass of whiskey to his lips.

One of the most important things I learned was that I wasn't alone. Jackie said that there were 28 million kids whose parents were alcoholics. I couldn't believe that there were 28 million kids of alcoholic parents! It made me feel better just to know that it wasn't just Mitch and me.

She also said that one-third of those kids would become alcoholics themselves. There were second and third and even fourth generation alcoholics. It really scared me to think that it would be easy for me to become an alcoholic. I could inherit the tendency from my dad.

There were slogans, too. One was *Easy Does It,* and another was *First Things First.* Each slogan seemed to make a little bit of sense when I thought about my dad and our family. At the end of the meeting, we all held hands and recited the Serenity Prayer:

God grant me the serenity to accept the things I cannot change, the courage to change the things I can, and the wisdom to know the difference. Everyone held another's hand.

After our meeting, I went back upstairs to meet Mom. She hugged me and asked how I liked the meeting. "I learned a lot, Mom," I answered. "I think Mitch should come next time. He's afraid of turning out like Dad." Jackie overheard me and stopped.

"That's a good idea, Darcy," she said.

On the way home, I asked Mom, "Did you have a hard time admitting that Dad was an alcoholic?"

"Yes, honey, I did." Mom took a deep breath. "I kept denying that your dad had a problem. I thought that if I refused to admit it, the problem might just go away. But it didn't."

When we got inside our house, Dad was passed out on the couch. Mom covered him with a blanket, but she didn't wake him. I felt sorry for him, but I told myself that Mom was doing the right thing. Like they said at the meeting, I couldn't stop Dad from drinking. He was an adult. I had to let him live his own life.

When I got home from school the next day, Dad was waterproofing his logging boots. He was sitting in the kitchen. He was also drinking a glass of whiskey. There was a bottle on the table, and I noticed that it was less than half full. He had a weird look on his face.

"Did you look for work today, Dad?" I asked.

He took another swallow of whiskey and kept rubbing the grease into his boots. The smell of the grease mixed with the smell of the whiskey made me sort of sick.

"I'm not going to spend my life begging for a job," he muttered. "I've got my pride. I'm Rory Gallatin."

"I know who you are, and you don't have to beg. But maybe you could ask for one." I could tell he was in a rotten mood, as well as drunk. I didn't feel like arguing with him. I tried to think of what Mrs. Wheeler would say I should do in this situation. I just walked out of the kitchen.

I went up to my room and tossed my books on the bed. Something looked different. I couldn't figure out what it was, and then I saw it!

My Garfield bank was lying on its side on the shelf. The plastic seal was on the floor. I picked up the bank. It felt light. It was almost empty!

My money, my savings money was gone! I ran out of my room and crashed into Dad in the hallway. He was standing there, swaying and drinking whiskey straight out of the bottle.

"I borrowed some money, Darcy," he said. "I needed a drink. I'll pay you back when I get a job."

Ten

I couldn't believe it! *Did he need booze so badly that he was willing to steal from his own daughter? What kind of a father would do that?* I wondered.

"You thief! You stinking, dirty thief! I'd never steal, not even from you! Never!"

"Darcy!" Dad grabbed for me, but he missed.

I tore the whiskey bottle from his hand and ran into the kitchen. Then I started dumping the booze down the sink.

Dad yanked me around and pulled the bottle away from me. It still had about two inches in it. Then he lifted his hand like he was going to smack me.

"Go ahead, and hit me!" I cried. "You're nothing but a drunk!"

Dad let me go. I took one step back, and then another and another until I could reach behind me and grab the door knob.

"I hate you! And I'll hate you for the rest of my life!" I raced out the door and across the backyard.

"Darcy! Darcy!" he cried after me, but I kept on running. I wanted to keep running forever.

I ran through the darkness to the clinic and Dr. Fred. I felt like he would know what to do. Maybe I could live with him and Lynn for a while. *Make that forever,* I thought. I wasn't going home again, not ever.

I was sobbing when I ran through the door of the clinic. Dr. Fred was there alone. He handed me a tissue and sat me down on his office chair.

"What is it, Darcy? What's happened?" he asked.

"My dad's a rotten, stinking drunk," I blurted out between sobs. "And he's a thief!" I couldn't stop crying.

"Try to calm down, Darcy," Dr. Fred said. "Tell me what happened."

I took some deep breaths and started to feel a little better. I finally managed to get the whole story out. Dr. Fred listened carefully. When I was finished telling him about my bank and about Dad almost hitting me, he said firmly, "The first thing you have to know, Darcy, is that your dad is a sick man.

He has a disease. He's an alcoholic."

I started to protest, but suddenly I didn't feel like arguing about it anymore.

Dr. Fred went on. "He's sick, just like if he had cancer or pneumonia. Alcoholism is a disease. It's his disease that made him steal your money, just like pneumonia makes people cough."

"That's just what Jackie—I mean, Mrs. Wheeler—said," I blurted out.

Dr. Fred had a look in his eyes that I had never seen before in all the time I had known him. I wasn't sure that he had even heard me.

"Darcy," he said, "alcoholism makes people do things they would never do if they didn't have the sickness. I know."

"But...but how do you know, Dr. Fred? You don't drink. Lynn told me you don't," I said.

Dr. Fred sighed and raked a hand through his white hair.

"Darcy, I know because I'm a recovering alcoholic. I used to drink as much as your dad does now, maybe more. I haven't touched a drop for ten and a half years."

I just stared at Dr. Fred. I couldn't believe that this man I'd known for years once drank as much as my dad. Dr. Fred even called himself a recovering alcoholic.

"I have to be careful all the time. I still want a drink sometimes, but I know that I can't risk it. I have too much to lose. I've been lucky. You see, Darcy, there is no cure for this disease. I'll always be an alcoholic."

Dr. Fred's eyes were red. "The worst thing of all about being an alcoholic is that I didn't care when my wife walked out on me and Lynn. I just kept drinking," he said.

Then I thought of something. "So, Lynn doesn't even know? She thinks you don't drink. She said when her mom left you just worked harder here at the clinic," I said.

"Lynn was only a baby when all of that happened. She doesn't remember. I've never told her about it. I don't want her to hate me because I drove her mother away," he said.

"Why did you quit drinking, Dr. Fred?" I asked.

He sat down. "I always used to have a few drinks to start work and a few drinks to unwind at the end of the day. One cold, rainy Sunday in the middle of winter, I had been drinking all day, and Evelyn Craig called. She had a colt that was sick with colic. You know that Mrs. Craig never calls unless it's a real emergency."

I nodded.

"I didn't go," Dr. Fred explained. "Evelyn

kept calling me, and I kept saying that I was on my way. And I went right on drinking. I didn't want to go out in the freezing drizzle. I never got up to go out there. I knew that I had a messy, muddy job ahead of me, and I just didn't feel like going. So, I just went on drinking."

"What happened?" My voice was only a whisper.

"You know that when a horse has colic, he gets down and rolls around trying to ease the pain in his stomach."

"I know," I said.

"Gas and fluid kept building up in the horse's stomach, until the stomach ruptured. That's how the colt died," he explained.

"Why didn't Mrs. Craig get another veterinarian if she knew that you weren't coming?" I asked.

"She trusted me," Dr. Fred said. "She thought that I'd be there. When she found out that I wasn't coming, she did call somebody else. But it was too late. The horse died in terrible pain."

He took off his glasses and rubbed his eyes. He continued, "She came to see me that evening. I was falling-down drunk. She gave me a shovel and told me I had a horse to bury. I did, Darcy. I buried him."

I heard rain starting on the roof of the clinic. Dr. Fred looked up. I could tell he was thinking about that night in the rain so long ago.

"The rain got worse that night, and it was cold. I kept falling in the mud. The hole filled up with water. And that horse's eyes were open. They were staring back at me, asking me why I never came to help."

"You quit drinking after that," I said. I knew it was true. He didn't have to tell me.

We sat there in the stillness, listening to the rain on the roof. Finally, Dr. Fred said to me softly, "Why don't you go home now, Darcy. Go and see how your dad is doing. I'm sure he feels just terrible. Maybe this incident will be for him what burying that horse was for me."

Walking home through the rain, I thought about everything that Dr. Fred had told me. I shivered when I thought about that dead horse's eyes staring up at him in the rain and mud. Then I thought, *If having Dad steal my money is what it takes for him to stop drinking, then he's welcome to it. I'd give all the money in the world if my dad would just get better.*

Eleven

IT was late when I got home, and the house was quiet. That was unusual for a Friday night. Someone was usually watching TV, or playing records or something. I didn't want to see anyone or talk to anyone, so I went straight up to my room.

I lay in my bed listening to the rain fall on the roof, and I thought about everything that Dr. Fred had told me. When I finally fell asleep, I had bad dreams. My dreams were a weird mix of a lot of the things that I had seen and heard in the last few weeks. In one of my dreams, Dave was offering Mitch a drink of his moonshine, and Mitch was just crying. But his crying sounded like the whimpering of the little dog that was hit by the truck. In another dream was Chief Johnson's police car, except that Scott was driving it. And in one dream was Dr. Fred's dead horse, staring up at me with those terrible eyes, and Dad was standing next to me.

When I woke up, the sun was shining through my window. The rain and clouds were gone, and the sun felt warm. I blinked a few times in the brightness. Then I saw that Mom and Dad were sitting on the edge of my bed. They were holding hands. Dad looked kind of bleary-eyed.

"Mom, Dad, what are you guys doing here? What time is it?" I asked, rubbing my eyes. I sat up in my bed.

"It's late. Your Dad has something to tell you, Darcy," answered Mom. She smiled at Dad.

Dad looked down at my bedspread for a moment. Then he looked up at me. "Darcy," he said slowly, "I know that I've been very bad to you. I've been bad to everyone I love. It just seems that the more I love you, the more I do to hurt you."

I tried to say something, but my voice wouldn't produce any words.

"Taking your money was a terrible thing to do. I'm sorry. It's not easy for me to say I'm sorry, Darcy," Dad continued. "I've always been so rough and tough that saying I'm sorry for things just isn't very easy for me. You have to understand, Darcy, that every time

I did something that hurt you or Mom or Mitch, it just made me hate myself even more. I knew that I was hurting you, and I had to drink even more to make me forget all the terrible things I did to you."

Dad stopped and wiped his eyes with his bandanna. I had never seen him cry before. Dad took my hand.

"I love you," he said. "I loved you the first minute I saw you as a baby in the hospital when you were born. When they let me hold you, I was afraid that I'd drop you. Then you smiled at me."

I started to cry when Dad talked about me as a baby. Dad stood up and walked over to the window. Mom stayed on the bed and said, "Darcy, Dr. Fred stopped by this morning and said that you went to the clinic last night. He told us everything."

I didn't know what to say. Then Dad came back to my side. He took a deep breath and said, "Darcy, I'm going to quit drinking. I used to think that drinking made me a big man, the toughest guy in Stilly. Now I know that it made me the smallest, the worst man. Nobody but the worst man would do to his family what I've done to mine. But you guys stuck with me, even when I didn't deserve it."

"Don't say that, Dad," I said between sobs.

I was crying my eyes out by this time. So were Mom and Dad. All of a sudden, Happy jumped up into the middle of the sobbing mess and started to lie down between us. Well, this made us all start laughing while we were still crying.

"Dad," I said, "we stuck by you because we're a family. That's what families are for, sticking together when times are tough."

Dad smiled. "Well, it's still more than I deserved, Darcy," he said. "But I'm going to try to do more to deserve it. Roaring Rory's going to be the best father in Stilly Falls!"

That made me laugh more, because it sounded just like my Dad, to always want to be the best. I think he thought the same thing, because he started laughing, too. "I guess that sounds just like me, always bragging about how I'm the best," he said.

Just then, Mitch came into my room. He must have heard the laughing and wondered what was going on. He almost sat down on Happy, who let out a yowl. "Isn't it great about Dad quitting drinking, Darce?" Mitch asked. "They told me about it this morning."

"I'm going to go to Alcoholics Anonymous," Dad said. "It's going to be the hardest thing I've ever done. Cutting down an eight-foot tree is nothing, compared to what I'll have to do there. That's why you all have to help me. I don't think I can do it myself."

"You won't be doing it yourself, Rory," Mom said quietly. "You know there's us, and Fred, too." She turned to me and Mitch. "Dr. Fred's going to be Dad's sponsor at AA. He's been through it, so he knows what we're up against."

"What do you mean, *we*, Mom?" asked Mitch.

"She means *we*, because we have to help Dad fight it," I answered. "It's all of our problem."

"Well," Dad said as he stood up, "like AA says, *we'll* just have to take it one day at a time."

I remembered what I told Mitch when he said he was going to stay away from alcohol. "I have faith in you, Dad," I told him. "I know you won't let us down, or let yourself down."

He gave me a great big smile.

Just then, we heard a knocking at the back door.

"Mitch," said Mom, "run down, and see who it is."

Mitch came back in a minute and said, "Darcy, it's Scott. He wants to know if you want to go build a dam down at the creek. He says there's a lot of water in the creek from the rain last night."

"I haven't built a dam since fourth grade!" I blurted out. *That Scott,* I thought.

"Why don't you go, Darcy?" suggested Mom. "You know what they say about all work and no play."

"Well, I guess my homework can wait," I said. "And it *is* perfect weather for building a dam. What is it they say at Alateen? Easy does it?"

Maybe we all ought to take it easy, I thought, *including me. I guess there's plenty of time to do my homework. There's plenty of time to be a veterinarian, to be grown-up Darcy Gallatin. I'll try to remember to take things one day at a time, too.*

"Okay, you guys!" I shouted as I jumped up. "Get out of here, so I can get dressed. Mitch, go tell Scott that I'll be right down!"

THE TWELVE STEPS OF ALATEEN

1. We admitted that we were powerless over alcohol–that our lives had become unmanageable.
2. Came to believe that a power greater than ourselves could restore us to sanity.
3. Made a decision to turn our will and our lives over to the care of God *as we understood Him.*
4. Made a searching and fearless moral inventory of ourselves.
5. Admitted to God, to ourselves, and to another human being the exact nature of our wrongs.
6. Were entirely ready to have God remove all these defects of character.
7. Humbly asked *Him* to remove our shortcomings.
8. Made a list of all persons we had harmed and became willing to make amends to them all.
9. Made direct amends to such people whenever possible, except when to do so would injure them or others.
10. Continued to take personal inventory, and when we were wrong promptly admitted it.
11. Sought through prayer and meditation to improve our conscious contact with God *as we understood Him,* praying only for knowledge of His will for us and the power to carry that out.
12. Having had a spiritual awakening as the result of these steps, we tried to carry these messages to others, and to practice these principles in all our affairs.

SLOGANS OF ALATEEN

Easy Does It
Slow up a little; think before you speak or act.

First Things First
No matter how many problems you have, you can only handle one at a time. Concentrate on each in turn. You'll get more done that way.

Let Go and Let God
We do our best with a problem, and then try to leave the results up to a Higher Power. Gaining confidence that things will work out for the best, helps us to stop worrying.

Live and Let Live
Live your own life the best way you can, and let other people do the same. Hold back on criticizing. Try not to hurt anybody in word or deed. This helps you build real strength of character.

About the Author

As a young girl, SHANNON KENNEDY'S favorite place to dream away the days was in an old cherry tree on her family's pony farm. Shannon read many books in that tree and in the hayloft of an old barn.

Today, Shannon lives with her mother on a ranch nestled in the foothills of the Cascade Mountains in Washington state. Her town is a little like Stilly Falls in *There's No Cure*. The ranch keeps Shannon pretty busy during the day, so she does most of her writing at night.

Shannon started writing in high school because the books she wanted to read hadn't been written yet. Shannon likes books about girls who do things–and Shannon has done some pretty impressive things herself. She drew on her experiences in the U.S. Army for her previous book *Daddy, Please Tell Me What's Wrong*.

When she's not writing, Shannon enjoys taking pictures, riding horses, and having fun with her 4-H club, the Horse Country Top Hands.